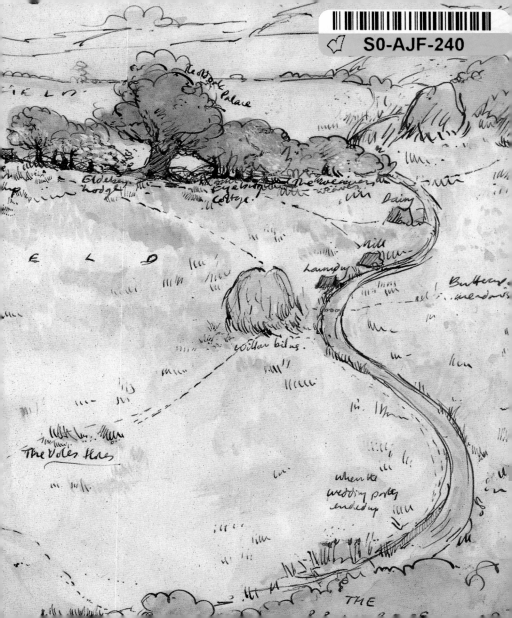

# SEA STORY

## Jill Barklem

HarperCollins *Children's Books*

# For my parents

For more information visit the Brambly Hedge website at:
www.bramblyhedge.com

First published in Great Britain by
HarperCollins Publishers Ltd in 1990
New edition published in 1996
This edition published by HarperCollins Children's Books in 2014

5 7 9 10 8 6

ISBN: 978-0-00-184563-3

HarperCollins Children's Books is a division of HarperCollins Publishers Ltd.

Visit our website at: www.harpercollins.co.uk

Printed and bound in China

# Brambly Hedge

For many generations, families of mice have made
their homes in the roots and trunks
of the trees of Brambly Hedge,
a dense and tangled hedgerow
that borders the field on the
other side of the stream.

The Brambly Hedge mice lead
busy lives. During the fine weather,
they collect flowers, fruits, berries and nuts from the
Hedge and surrounding fields, and prepare
delicious jams, pickles and preserves that
are kept safely in the Store Stump for
the winter months ahead.

Although the mice work hard, they make
time for fun too. All through the year, they
mark the seasons with feasts and festivities and, whether
it be a little mouse's birthday, an eagerly awaited wedding
or the first day of spring, the mice
welcome the opportunity
to meet and celebrate.

Primrose woke early that summer morning. She dressed quickly and tiptoed down to the kitchen. Her mother was already up, packing a rain cloak and hat into a small bag.

"Off you go," she said. "Take this apple to eat on the way. We'll see you later to say goodbye."

Outside the sun was already warm, and a light breeze stirred the leaves and branches of Brambly Hedge.

"Perfect," said Primrose, "just right for an adventure."

She ran across the field, through the long grass and down to the stream. There she found Dusty, Poppy and Wilfred hard at work, loading provisions on to Dusty's boat.

"Here you are at last," said Dusty, "I was beginning to think we'd have to leave you behind."

Wilfred helped Primrose carry her bag down the steep wooden steps to the cabin below.

"Look at this!" he said, pointing to an ancient yellow map spread out on the chart table.

"Does it show where we're going?" she asked.

"Yes," said Dusty, "it's the old Salters' map. Here's our hedge, and we've got to sail all the way down this river," he pointed to a wiggly blue line, "to the sea!"

On the bank a small crowd of mice had gathered to see them off.

"Will they be all right?" asked Mrs Apple anxiously. "Dusty's never sailed so far before."

"Look, my dear," said Mr Apple, "if the sea mice can manage to get the salt all the way up to us, I'm sure Dusty can sail downstream to fetch it."

"I can't think why we've run out," said Mrs Apple. "It's never happened before. Perhaps I shouldn't have salted all those walnuts."

"Stop worrying," said Mr Apple. "Look, they're about to leave."

"All aboard?" called Dusty. He hoisted the sail, cast off and turned the *Periwinkle* into the current. The voyage was about to begin.

The fresh breeze took them quickly downstream. Primrose and Wilfred stood by the rail and waved until everyone was out of sight, and then ran to explore the boat.

They each chose a bunk, Primrose the top one, Wilfred the one below, and stowed away their toys and clothes. Then they hurried back up to help Dusty with the sails.

Poppy prepared a picnic lunch which they ate on deck, watching the trees and riverbanks as they passed by.

"The wind's getting up," said Dusty, as he cleared away, "make sure that everything's secure." At that moment the boat began to heel to one side, and an apple bounced to the floor.

"Can I steer?" Wilfred asked.

"Not in this wind, old chap."

"We're going rather fast," said Poppy.

"Yes, we'll be there in no time," said Dusty cheerfully, hauling in on the ropes.

All afternoon the boat sped along, past rushes, trees and fields.

"Look out for a sheltered spot where we can moor up for the night," said Dusty. "I don't like the look of that sky."

"Will this do?" asked Poppy as they rounded a bend in the stream. Dusty turned the *Periwinkle* in towards the bank, and Poppy threw a rope around a twisted root to make it fast.

They were all glad to go below deck to get warm. Poppy lit the lamps, and heated some soup on the stove.

After supper, they sat round the table telling stories and singing songs until it was time for bed. The children, tired after all the fresh air, snuggled happily into their bunks. Outside, the water lapped the sides of the boat, and rocked them gently to sleep.

Next morning, Primrose woke to the sound of
the wind rushing through the willows on the bank.
Poppy was already up, making toast. Dusty and
Wilfred were at the chart table, studying the map.

"You'll need to dress warmly today," said Poppy.

Soon the sails were up and they were on their
way again. Wilfred helped Dusty on deck, and
Primrose looked out for landmarks for Poppy to
find on the map.

The day went quickly as the boat skimmed along
down the river. By tea time the children had decided
to become explorers.

"Look out! Sea Weasels!"
shouted Wilfred.

He jumped into the cockpit,
tripped over a rope, and knocked the
tiller from Dusty's paw. Dusty grabbed for it, but
too late – the boat swung round and headed for
the bank. There was a dreadful scraping noise and
the boat stopped dead. They had run aground.

"We'll *never* get to the sea now," wailed Primrose.
Wilfred hung his head; he felt close to tears.

"Sorry, Dusty," he muttered.

"We won't get off this evening," sighed Dusty,
trying to lever the boat away with an oar. "We'd
better go below and have supper."

The sound of heavy rain greeted the mice next morning. When Dusty looked through the porthole he saw that the water level had risen during the night and floated them clear.

"Hooray," he shouted, and dashed up on deck to take the tiller. "Fetch the map; I think we're nearly there."

Primrose pointed ahead. "Look, that must be Seagull Rock. I can see some boats."

As they drew closer, they saw some water shrews fishing on the bank.

Dusty cupped his paws. "Are we on course for Sandy Bay?" he called.

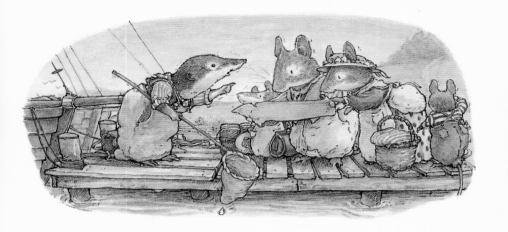

"Best anchor here and take the path up to the cliffs," said the water shrew.

Dusty moored up neatly between the other boats and the four mice stepped ashore. Slowly they made their way up the steep path through the pine trees.

At last they stepped up to the very brow of the hill, and there, spread out before them, glittering in the afternoon sun, was…

…the sea.

"It's so big!" gasped Primrose.

"And so blue!" added Wilfred.

One after another, clutching at tufts of marram grass for support, they slithered down the path.

"Which way now?" asked Primrose.

Dusty looked at the map. "To the right," he said, "past the sea campions."

Poppy was the first one to catch sight of a group of mice sitting by a door in the sandy cliffs.

"Excuse me," she called, "we're looking for Purslane Saltapple."

"Well, that's me!" replied one of the mice.

Dusty, delighted, ran to shake his paw. "We're from Brambly Hedge," he explained. "We've run out of salt."

"Then it's a fair wind that blew you here," said Purslane. "Let me introduce my wife Thrift, and our children Pebble, Shell and baby Shrimp."

"You must be exhausted," said Thrift. "Come inside, do, and make yourselves comfortable. I expect you'd like to wash your paws."

She led them down a passage to the bathroom. "This is the water for washing," she said, pointing to a pitcher on the floor. "If you'd like a drink, come along to the kitchen."

Poppy and Dusty's bedroom looked straight onto the sea. Primrose and Wilfred were to sleep in the nursery.

Poppy left them to unpack and went to find
Thrift. She was busy in the kitchen, rinsing some
brown fronds in a colander.

"Have you ever tasted seaweed?" she asked.

"No," Poppy replied, "but I'm sure it will be very
interesting to try it."

Soon they were sitting round the table, and trying their first taste of seaside food.

"What's this?" asked Wilfred warily, prodding the pile of vegetables on his plate.

"Marsh samphire, of course," said Pebble.

"Do I have to eat it?" whispered Wilfred.

Poppy coughed and quickly asked, "How long have the Saltapples been here, Purslane?"

"Our family has lived in this dune for generations. A long, long time ago our ancestors left the Green Fields and settled here. We've never been back, and I've often wondered what it's like."

At this, they began to tell each other about their very different lives in the hedgerow and by the sea.

"I've brought you a few things from Brambly Hedge," said Poppy, fetching her basket. Mrs Apple's honeycakes and strawberry jelly tasted strangely sweet to the Sea Mice, and the candied violets had to be put out of the baby's reach.

"Bedtime, children," said Thrift. "If it's fine, we'll go to the beach tomorrow."

   As soon as they were up, the children wanted to go
straight to the sea.
   "You'd better wear sunhats," said Thrift. "It's going
to be hot. We'll take a picnic and spend the day there."

   While Pebble and Wilfred built a sand palace,
Shell and Primrose hunted for treasure in the rock
pools, and Shrimp raced along the shore, getting in
everyone's way.

   The grown-ups spread out the picnic cloth, and
reminisced about friends and relations as they
watched the children play.

   Suddenly, Poppy noticed that the waves were
starting to creep up the beach, and she called the
children back to the dune.

   "It's the tide," explained Purslane. "It goes out
and comes in twice every day. Soon the beach will
be covered with water. It's time to go home."

On the third day, Wilfred woke to see dark clouds rolling in over the sea. Purslane hurried past the nursery door, pulling on his waterproofs.

"I've got to get the salt pans covered before the storm breaks," he cried. "Come and help!"

They ran through a tunnel to the back of the dune and out into the rising wind. Purslane paused to hoist up a red flag, and they scrambled down through the rough grass to the salt marsh. Wilfred could see two huge dishes in the ground. One of them was covered and the other open to the sky.

Purslane ran to release a lever and struggled to push the cover from one dish to the other.

"What's in here?" shouted Wilfred.

"We put seawater in one pan," said Purslane, "the sun dries up the water and leaves the salt for us to collect. The other one is to catch rainwater for us to drink."

Just as they finished lashing down the cover, the rain swept in from the sea. By the time they got home, huge waves were crashing on to the beach, and spray spattered against the windows.

It was dark inside the house. Thrift lit the fire in the nursery and trimmed the lamp.

"Sometimes we have to stay in for days and days," said Shell.

"Especially in the winter," added Pebble.

The children played dominoes and five stones
and made pictures with seaweed.

Pebble helped Wilfred make a little boat with real
sails and rigging, and Primrose painted a beautiful
stone mouse as a present for her mother.

The storm blew itself out in the night. As soon as he got up, Purslane felt the seaweed by the front door and held up his paw to check the wind.

"It's set fair for your journey home," he said.

"Then I think we should be off as soon as we can," said Dusty.

"We must fetch the salt up from the store," said Purslane. "Will three barrels be enough?"

While their parents were busy, the children went off to play hide-and-seek in the maze of tunnels under the dune. They hid in storerooms full of pungent seaweed, behind jars of pickles and roots, and heaps of glistening shells.

"Let's go down to the storm bunker," said Pebble when he had found them all. He led them to some cold dark rooms deep in the heart of the dune.

"We come down here when it gets really rough," said Shell. "It's safer."

"Where are you?" called Thrift faintly. "It's time to leave."

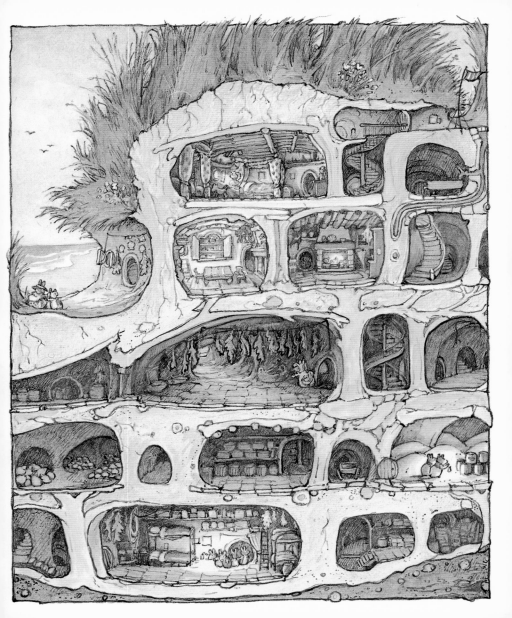

Reluctantly, Primrose and Wilfred went to the
nursery to collect their things. Wilfred tied his boat
to his haversack and put his collection of stones in
his pocket. Primrose stood and gazed out of the
window. "I don't want to go home," she said.

"We've a present for you," said Pebble quickly.
"This is your special shell. Every time you hold it to
your ear, you'll hear the sound of the sea and that
will remind you to come and see us again."

Dusty and Purslane loaded the barrels of salt on
to a handcart, and laden down with luggage and
gifts, the little party set off along the dune.

They scrambled down the cliff path to the *Periwinkle* and with some difficulty loaded everything on board.

"Keep that salt dry, mind," said Purslane.

"Try and visit us one day," said Poppy. "We'd like to show you Brambly Hedge."

"All aboard!" called Dusty.

"And no stowaways," added Poppy, lifting Shrimp out of a basket.

They hugged their new friends goodbye, and thanked them for all their help. Poppy loosened the mooring ropes and Dusty hoisted the sail. He steered the boat into the stream once more and Primrose and Wilfred waved until Shell and Pebble were out of sight.

> *"I'm a salter on the salty sea*
> *A' sailing on the foam,*
> *But the salter's life is the sweetest*
> *When the sail is set for home,"*

sang Wilfred as a fresh breeze caught the sails and swept them round a bend in the river.